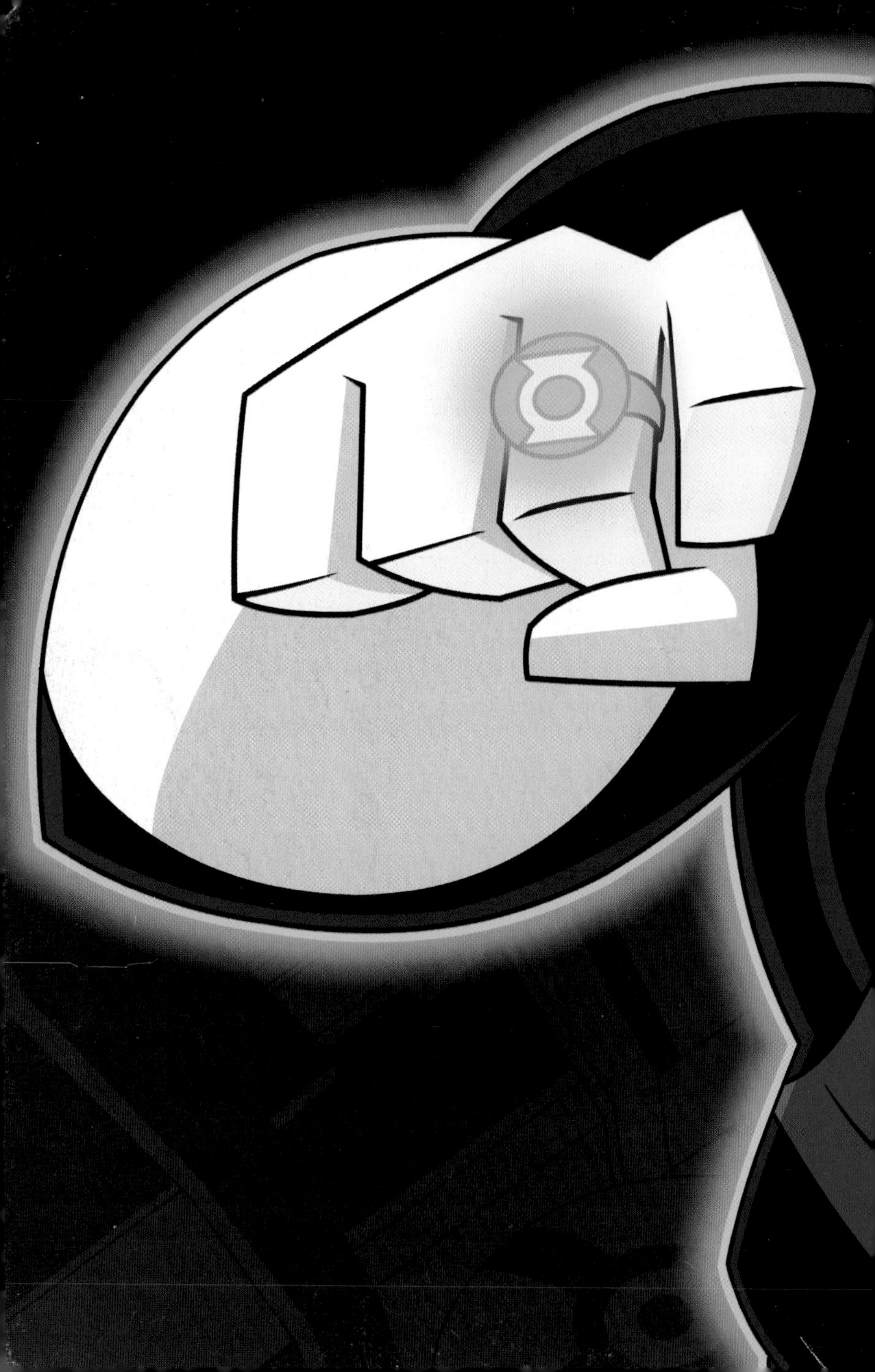

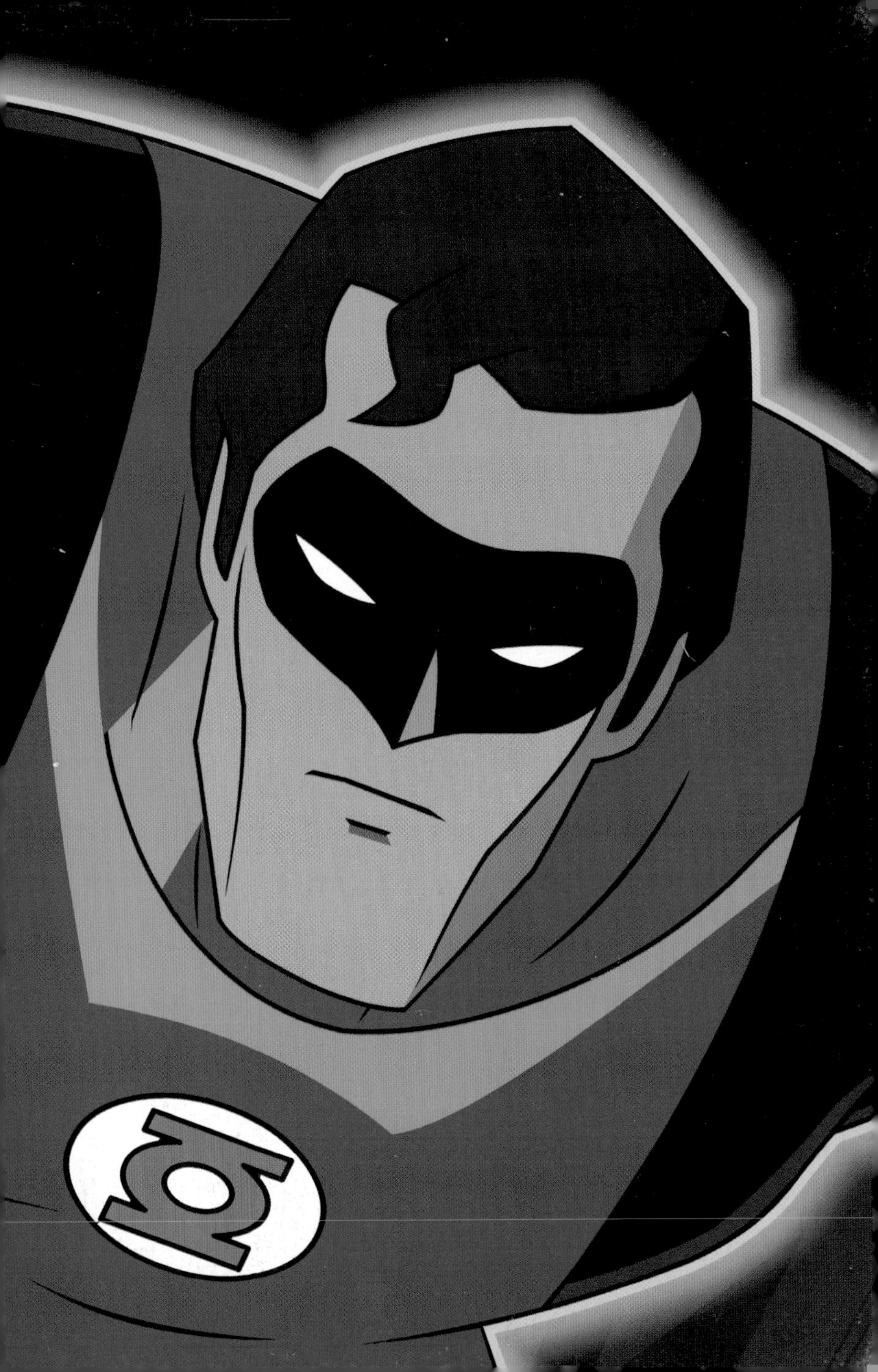

...ALACTIC PEACEKEEPING
...CORPS, HAL JORDAN
...UNIFORM AND RING OF . . .

DC HEROES

GREEN LANTERN

SAVAGE SANDS

WRITTEN BY
J.E. BRIGHT

ILLUSTRATED BY
DAN SCHOENING

STONE ARCH BOOKS
a capstone imprint

Published by Stone Arch Books in 2012
A Capstone Imprint
151 Good Counsel Drive, P.O. Box 669
Mankato, Minnesota 56002
www.capstonepub.com

Library of Congress Cataloging-in-Publication Data
Bright, J. E.
  Savage sands / written by J.E. Bright ; illustrated by Dan Schoening.
    p. cm. -- (DC super heroes)
  ISBN-13: 978-1-4342-2619-8 (library binding)
  ISBN-13: 978-1-4342-3405-6 (pbk.)
  1. Green Lantern (Fictitious character)--Juvenile fiction. 2. Superheroes--
Juvenile fiction. 3. Supervillains--Juvenile fiction. 4. Great Sphinx (Egypt)-
-Juvenile fiction. 5. Mummies--Juvenile fiction. 6. Egypt--Juvenile fiction.
[1. Superheroes--Fiction. 2. Supervillains--Fiction. 3. Great Sphinx (Egypt)--
Fiction. 4. Mummies--Fiction. 5. Egypt--Fiction.] I. Schoening, Dan, ill. II.
Title.
  PZ7.B76485Sav 2012
  813.6--dc22   2011005154

Summary: The immortal super-villain Vandal Savage is loose! He has escaped
prison and fled to the timeless tombs of Egypt, where he raises an army of
living mummies. Hal Jordan, as Green Lantern, soars into the shifting sands
to defeat the zombie-like rampage, but Vandal Savage has another weapon. He
animates the sleeping Sphinx itself! Hal must solve the ancient riddle of the
stone-cold creature, or he'll never leave Egypt alive.

Art Director: Bob Lentz and Brann Garvey
Designer: Hilary Wacholz
Production Specialist: Michelle Biedscheid

Printed in the United States of America in Stevens Point, Wisconsin.
082011
006341R

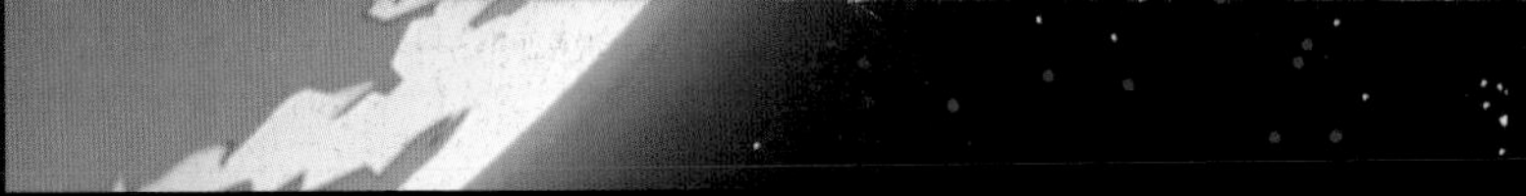

TABLE OF CONTENTS

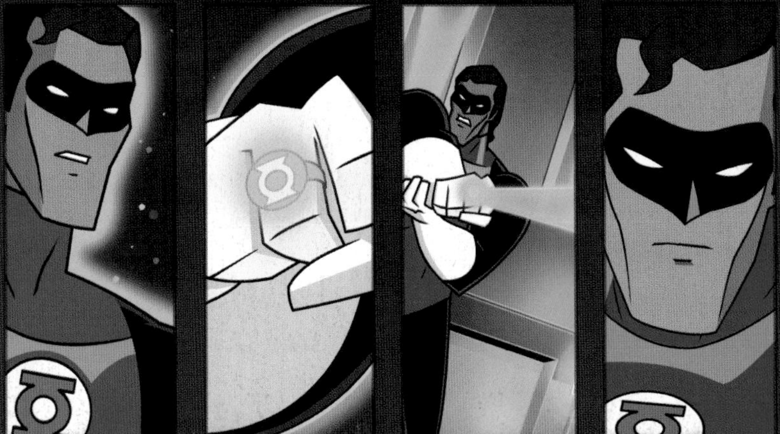

CHAPTER 1

VANDAL ON VIDEO

ZWWMOOOMMMM!

Test pilot Hal Jordan scorched through the sky above Edwards Air Force Base. He was flying in an experimental X-211 hypersonic scramjet.

The X-211 was shaped more like a rocket than a plane. Hal piloted from a tiny space in the nose cone, controlling flexible metal fins along the sides to steer. The craft couldn't use standard wings. They could never withstand the shock waves of its faster-than-sound speed.

The engineers at the base had designed the aircraft to reach Mach 7. No jet in history had accomplished this daring feat. And nobody had ever successfully landed in an X-211 before. Hal was determined to be the first to succeed at both.

High over the California desert, the X-211 zoomed westward, trembling as it picked up speed. The stony landscape whipped beneath it in a blur.

Hal smiled in his oxygen mask as the aircraft shuddered from a sonic boom. He loved breaking the sound barrier. Hal accelerated again, aiming higher into thinner atmosphere. The maneuver would lessen the friction drag on the craft.

"All clear for full speed," Colonel Sellers said to Hal over the radio.

"Roger that," Hal replied. It was time to find out what the X-211 could really do.

Hal gunned the engine. **WHAM!** The incredible g-force slammed him back into the specially cushioned seat. He grinned again. Hal loved nothing more than flying at speeds on the edge of what humans had previously achieved.

However, Hal had flown faster in his life. Secretly, he was Green Lantern. When using his special power ring, he could fly faster than light. But he was testing the X-211 for the safety of humans, not super heroes. And Hal felt an unusual thrill from flying without his superpowers.

The X-211 broke Mach 6. Hal could feel the ship's vibrations in his teeth.

Hal knew from experience that the rattling meant the aircraft wasn't going to hold together forever. It didn't have to. Hal just needed a few more moments to reach Mach 7, decelerate, and land.

"Almost there," Colonel Sellers squawked over the radio. "How's it holding together, Jordan?"

"I'll be honest," Hal replied. "It's pretty rough up here."

"Abort if necessary," ordered the colonel. "Don't take any crazy chances."

Hal joked back. "That doesn't sound like me —"

The X-211 rattled uncontrollably. Hal fought to straighten it out. "Seriously, Jordan!" Sellers squawked over the radio. "I don't like these readings!"

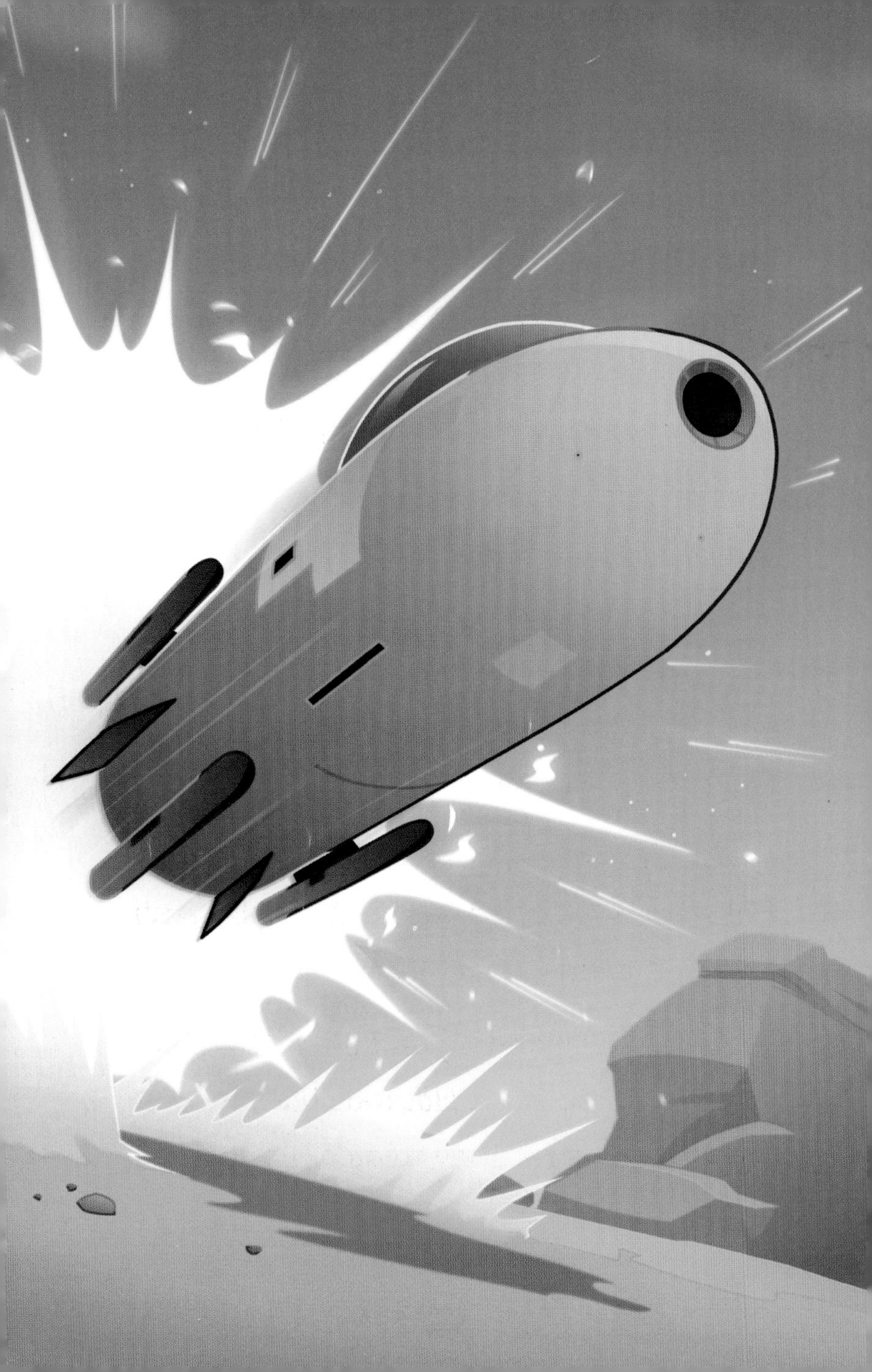

Hal could see from the control panel that he was seconds away from breaking Mach 7. "Going for it!" he grunted. If something went wrong, Hal could escape using his power ring, but until the last second, he would hold on. He just wasn't a fearful kind of guy.

Besides, he loved to fly.

BARROOOOOMMM

Gritting his teeth, Hal blasted through Mach 7. He'd done it!

Grinning at the cheers over the radio, Hal slowed down the X-211. He circled back toward the base.

After a safe landing on Rogers Dry Lake just outside the base, Hal rode back with the retrieval crew. They treated him like a hero, but Hal was used to that.

When Hal got back to the base, General Jonathan "Herc" Stone was waiting for him outside headquarters.

"Very impressive, Jordan," Herc said. "No time to celebrate, though. I've got something I need to show you. *Now.*"

"Sounds important," Hal replied, following the general into his office. Hal had a feeling Herc didn't need him as a test pilot. He needed him as Green Lantern. Herc knew that Hal was also a super hero and sometimes informed him about problems the military couldn't handle alone.

"Important enough for Green Lantern," General Stone whispered. He shut the door to his office behind Hal, and then swiveled the computer screen on his desk so Hal could see it.

"We've been sent a security camera video from the National Archeology Museum," General Stone said. "I thought you might recognize someone on it."

Hal looked at the grainy video images. He could make out the back of a tall, powerful man striding between glass cases in the museum's Ancient Egypt exhibit. The man headed straight for a huge stone sarcophagus.

The camera had picked up the screams of the museumgoers as the man easily ripped the lid off the sarcophagus. He tossed it aside. The stone lid shattered on the museum's marble floor.

"Well, he's strong," Hal commented.

"Very," Herc said with a grunt. "That lid weighs more than a ton."

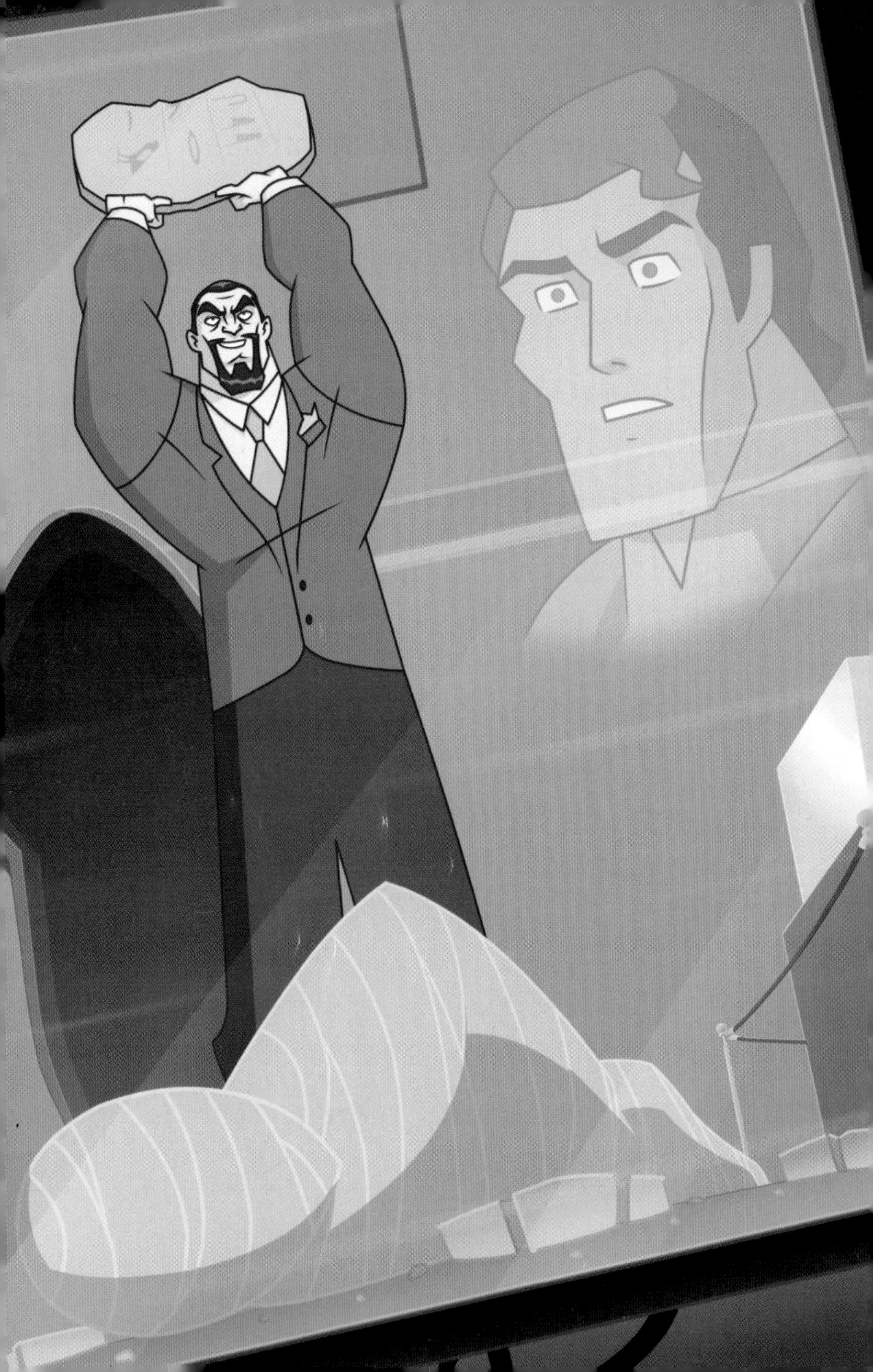

Then the man pulled the mummy out of the sarcophagus and dumped it on the floor. He reached into the stone casket and grabbed a fragment of a clay tablet.

"I am claiming what is rightfully mine!" the man declared, holding up the tablet.

Hal could see that it was etched with hieroglyphics, the writing of the ancient Egyptians.

The man turned around, smiled grimly, and stormed out of the museum.

Hal recognized the man instantly. "Vandal Savage," he groaned.

CHAPTER 2

THE SANDS OF EGYPT

Hal quickly explained to General Stone why it was bad news that Vandal Savage was once again on the loose. Savage was a Cro-Magnon man who had been given immortality by a mysterious meteor. He had been causing trouble on Earth for the last 50,000 years. The villain had ruled hundreds of evil civilizations throughout history. He was always searching for a new way to take over the world.

"Savage was even an advisor to Rā's al Ghūl — a notorious villain," Hal said.

"He's been the definition of a bad guy ever since there were bad guys," Hal added.

Herc nodded. "We've been getting reports of strange weather problems in the Egyptian desert," he said. "Huge sandstorms and such. They started the day after this guy broke into the Egyptian exhibit, so I figure there's a connection."

"No doubt," Hal replied. "There are rumors that Savage actually ruled Egypt as the Pharaoh Khafre around 2,500 B.C. He was supposed to have built one of the Great Pyramids, and the Sphinx, using brutal slave labor. He needs to be stopped."

Hal hurried out of Herc's office and strode through the base to the pilots' locker room. He kept his power battery in his work locker. It seemed like a good idea to recharge his ring before heading to Egypt.

After making sure nobody was around, Hal held his ring to the battery and recited his sacred oath:

"In brightest day,
In blackest night,
No evil shall escape my sight.
Let those who worship evil's might,
Beware my power —
Green Lantern's light!"

"Power levels at 100%," the ring reported to Hal.

Then Hal rushed outside and used the ring's power to soar into the sky.

WHOOOOSH!

He changed into his Green Lantern uniform just by thinking about it. As a Green Lantern, Hal could travel fast. It took him less than fifteen minutes to reach the Giza Plateau in Egypt.

What Green Lantern found in the Egyptian desert was total chaos. Wild swirls of sand whipped around the pyramids, forming an unbreakable ring around the area. Egyptian military vehicles were stopped on the edges of the whirling ring, partially buried by sand. This was no mere sandstorm. It was a sand hurricane.

Green Lantern dived into the center of the wind, which came from directly above the ancient Great Sphinx statue.

Even with his ring's energy protecting him, Green Lantern felt the powerful force of the storm.

It didn't help that the sand was yellow. For years, he had been powerless against the color yellow, but his power had evolved. Now he could affect yellow things if he accepted the fear he felt.

Summoning all his bravery, Green Lantern imagined a hurricane spinning out of his ring. Green winds swooped around him, twirling in the opposite direction of the sandstorm. He concentrated on strengthening his winds.

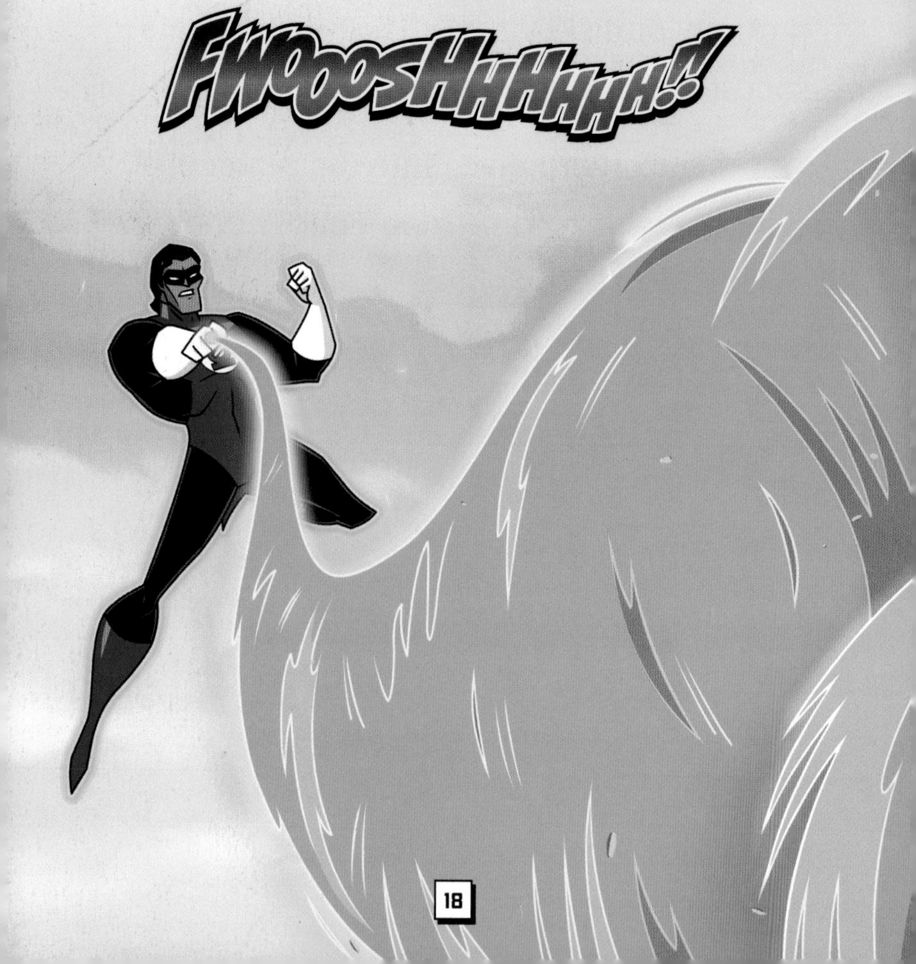
FWOOOSHHHHHH!!

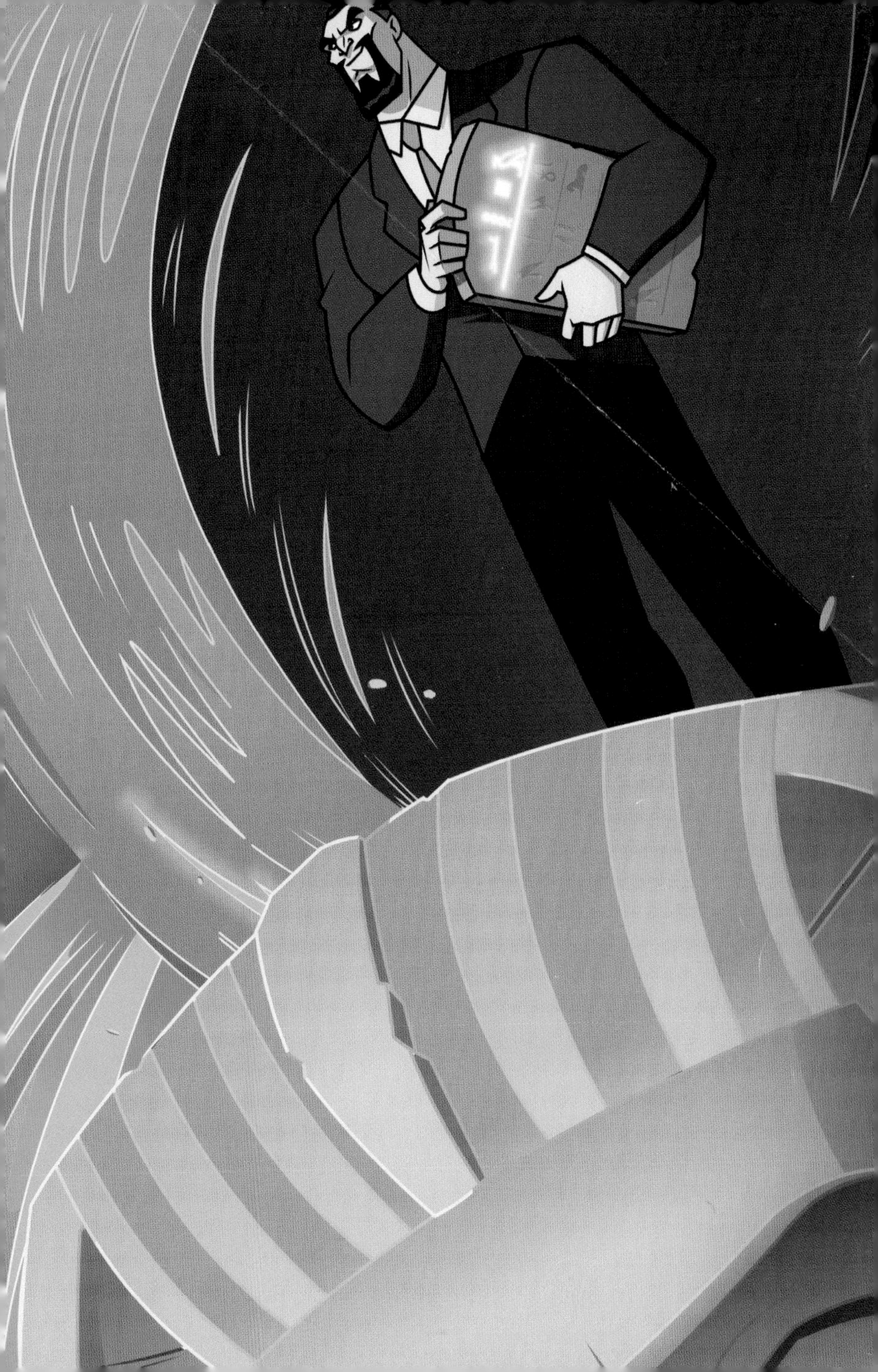

In moments, the two storms were balanced, and the sandstorm stopped. Loose sand snowed down on the desert below.

With the sky now clear, Green Lantern spotted Vandal Savage standing on the back of the Great Sphinx. He soared down to confront the villain.

"Surrender, Savage!" Green Lantern ordered, pointing his glowing ring at the villain. "I beat your sandstorm!"

Vandal Savage laughed and raised a stone tablet above his head.

Green Lantern could see that the tablet had been recently repaired. A jagged crack still ran through it.

"The sandstorm was just the beginning," Savage said.

"I wrote these words when I was tired of being Pharaoh, as a way of ensuring I could always raise an army if I needed one. My subjects thought I was dead and laid a fake body to rest under my pyramid, along with this tablet. Unfortunately, a piece was stolen, and it's taken me thousands of years to find it."

"That's what you stole from the museum!" Green Lantern said.

"Stole?" Savage repeated. "How can I steal what's mine? I wrote this tablet 4,500 years ago. Now that it's complete again, I'll use my army to conquer the world!"

Before Green Lantern could stop him, Savage quickly recited words in ancient Egyptian. The tablet glimmered with eerie yellow light.

A strange moaning noise echoed across the desert. All around the pyramids, the sand churned.

RUMMMMMMMMMBLE!

Then thousands of mummified warriors climbed out of the sands. They staggered toward their leader.

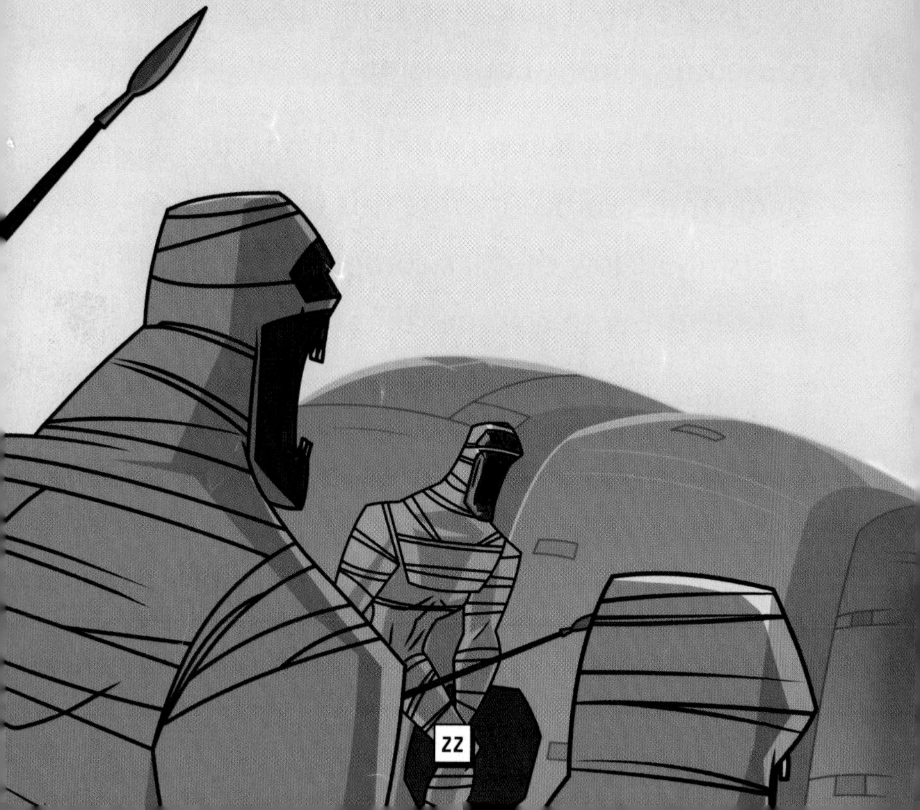

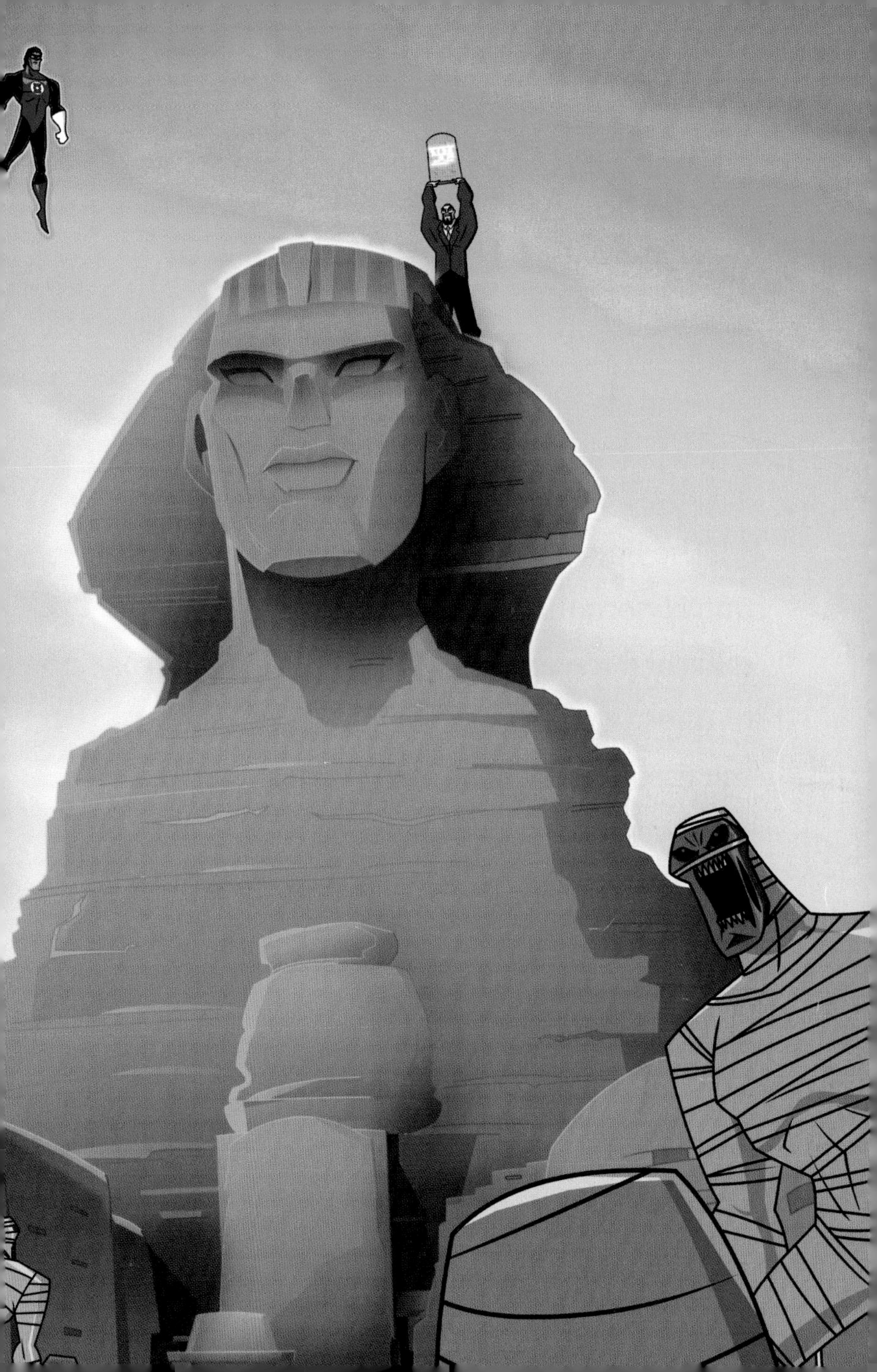

CHAPTER 3

ARMY OF THE UNDEAD

The enormous army of mummies quickly organized into rows as they marched toward the Sphinx. The legions of ghastly soldiers stretched back across the desert as far as Green Lantern could see. Each mummy was wrapped in ancient rags, and every one carried a rusty spear and a pentagon-shaped shield. All together, the mummies stopped and saluted Vandal Savage.

"My faithful slaves!" Savage cried. "Onward to victory!"

Vandal pointed to the city of Cairo beyond the pyramids. "March and destroy!" he said. "First Cairo, then the world!"

Green Lantern swooped in front of the marching mummies. They ignored him and kept stomping toward Cairo. He had to stop them somehow.

Aiming his power ring, Green Lantern let loose blast after blast into the legion of mummies. **WHAM! WHAM!** He hit some with huge energy fists, some with a giant glowing brick wall, some with green lightning bolts, and others with enormous cannon balls.

But there were two problems with fighting a vast army of mummies. First, there were just too many for any one man to defeat. Secondly, the mummies were already dead!

When Green Lantern knocked the creatures down, they just got up again. When he blew them apart with explosive blasts, their pieces crawled back together and in moments they were marching again.

"Ring," Green Lantern said, "how do you stop an army of undead?"

"Mummies are vulnerable to fire," the power ring answered.

He created a colossal magnifying glass and held it over the mummy army. By focusing the hot desert rays through the glass, Green Lantern sizzled hundreds of mummies at once.

"Fools!" Vandal Savage shouted at his undead soldiers. "He's destroying you! Overwhelm him!"

The mummies stopped marching and instead staggered toward Green Lantern. They stabbed at him with their spears. They surrounded him, grabbing his legs when he tried to fly away, pulling him down.

Green Lantern put up his force field, which protected him from the spears. But there were too many mummies attacking him and holding on to his limbs. He couldn't fight all of them at once.

The mummies piled onto Green Lantern, burying him under their rotting bodies. While he was held down, the rest of the army resumed their march toward Cairo.

Green Lantern struggled to blast his way free. He widened the range of his force field, which gave him some breathing room.

He had to think of a way to burn up the mummies more quickly than the magnifying glass had managed.

"To fight an ancient power," Green Lantern realized, "I need to use an ancient power. Even a mythological one!"

While holding his force field steady, Green Lantern constructed an immense dragon. Its massive green wings cast a shadow over half the mummy army.

Then Green Lantern made the dragon breathe green fire down on the mummies as it soared overhead.

With each pass, the dragon incinerated rows and rows of mummies. They crumbled into black ash on the sand. The dragon cleared the area around Green Lantern, and then went to work burning up the rest.

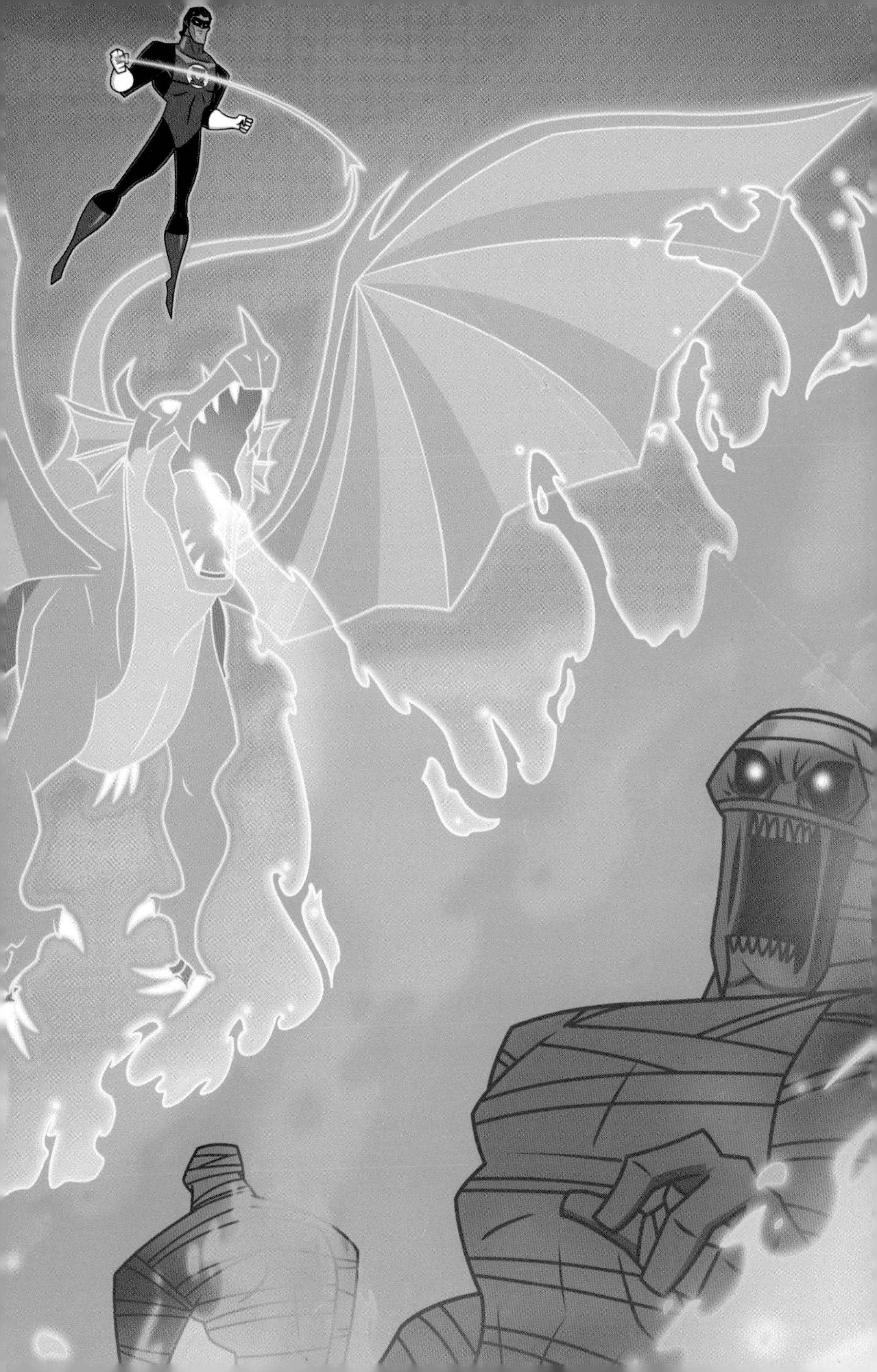

"Attack the dragon!" Savage cried. "Throw your spears!"

The remaining mummies regrouped and hurled their spears at the dragon, but there were too few of them left. Green Lantern steered the dragon across the desert, wiping out the mummies with blasts of fire. Soon, only a few stragglers were still standing.

"No!" Savage hollered. "It's not possible! You defeated my army!"

Green Lantern turned and faced Savage atop the Sphinx. "Give it up, Savage," he said. "You've lost."

Vandal Savage raised the tablet. "Not quite," he said. "I have a backup plan." Once again, the pictograms on the tablet shined with energy.

Then the Sphinx stood.

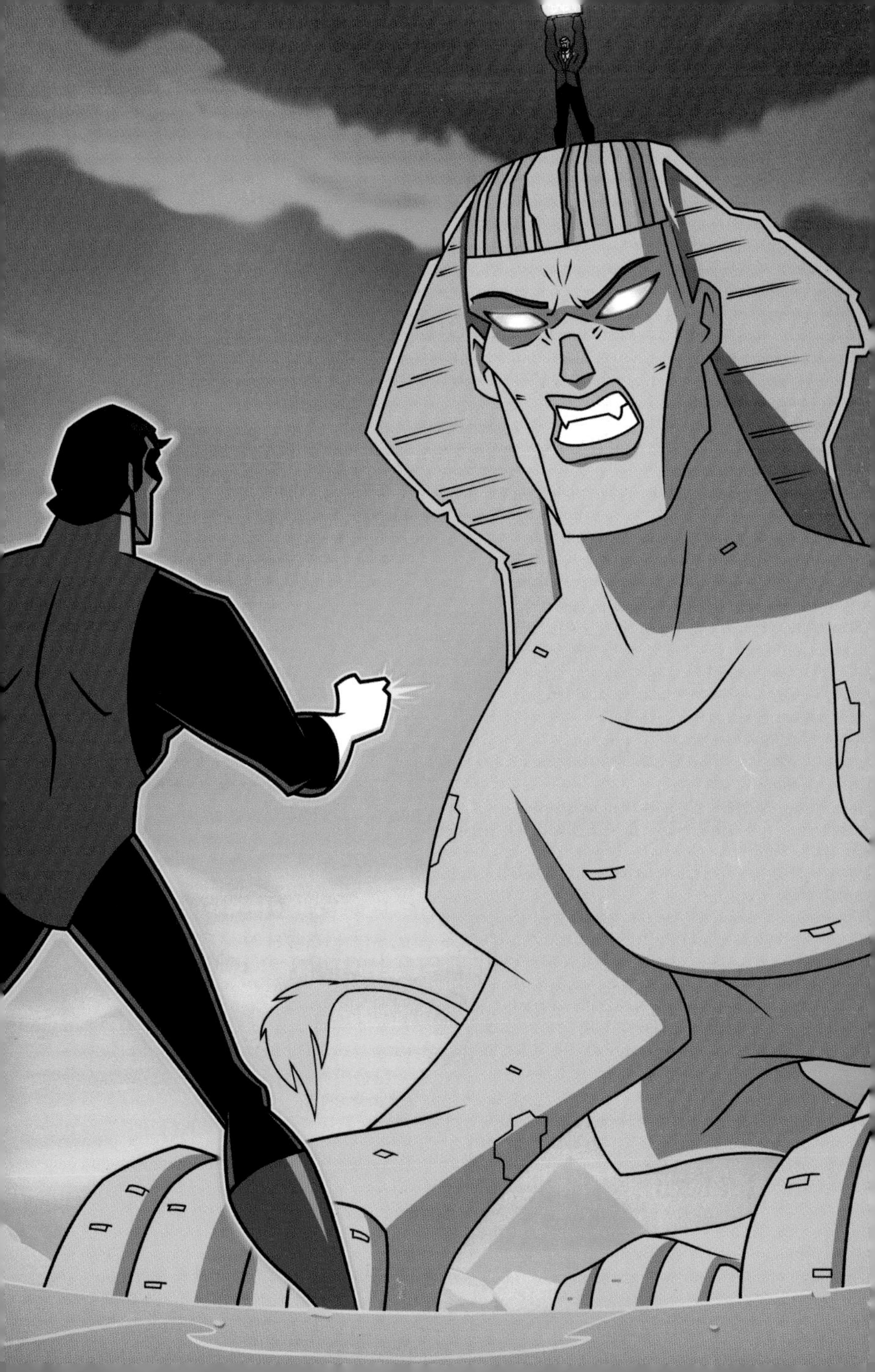

CHAPTER 4

THE SLEEPING GIANT

"When I had him built, his face looked just like mine!" Vandal Savage shouted from atop the Sphinx's back. "The years have taken their toll on his looks. However, I think you'll find he's as ruthless now as he was 4,500 years ago!"

The colossal creature roared at Green Lantern. The super hero leaped backward to avoid a swipe from the beast's huge claws. The Sphinx was enormous — more than 260 feet long, 20 feet wide, and 60 feet tall.

The monster was even taller standing up. Worst of all, he had been made from yellowish sandstone, which made him even harder for Green Lantern to fight.

"Attack!" Vandal Savage ordered the Sphinx. The villain dropped into a crouch on the creature's back, holding on tight.

The Sphinx pounced at Green Lantern. It was surprisingly quick for something of such immense size. Green Lantern barely had time to dart out of the way.

Time to finish this battle! the super hero thought.

Hovering in the air, Green Lantern aimed the strongest energy bolt he could imagine at the Sphinx.

THWOOOOMMMMMM!!

The Sphinx didn't even move.

The beast opened its mouth wide. It inhaled the sizzling energy bolt, closed his mouth, and smiled. The only effect that Green Lantern could see was that the Sphinx's yellow eyes glowed more brightly.

Savage laughed. "It's mystical energy that animates him," the villain said. "Your energy bolts just make him stronger!"

Green Lantern narrowed his eyes. If a direct attack wouldn't work, he would just have to get creative. With his ring, he constructed a giant hammer and chisel, concentrating on making the chisel's blade super-sharp. "Maybe this statue needs more sculpting!" the hero shouted.

Green Lantern sent the chisel toward the Sphinx's neck. As soon as it connected, Green Lantern whacked the handle of the chisel with the hammer. THWACK!

The Sphinx roared, but the chisel couldn't break its stony hide.

"Stupid super hero," Savage called. "The Sphinx is a being of pure energy." He clopped his heels against the Sphinx's sides. "Now it's our turn!"

The Sphinx crouched down and leaped up at Green Lantern, catching him in his paws like a cat. Green Lantern was knocked down onto the desert sand, squashed beneath the Sphinx's mitts. **THUD!**

"Let us show you why the word 'Sphinx' means 'strangler'!" Savage shouted.

The Sphinx closed his paws around Green Lantern and started crushing him. Green Lantern gasped for air, horrified that his force field wasn't protecting him from the monster's grasp.

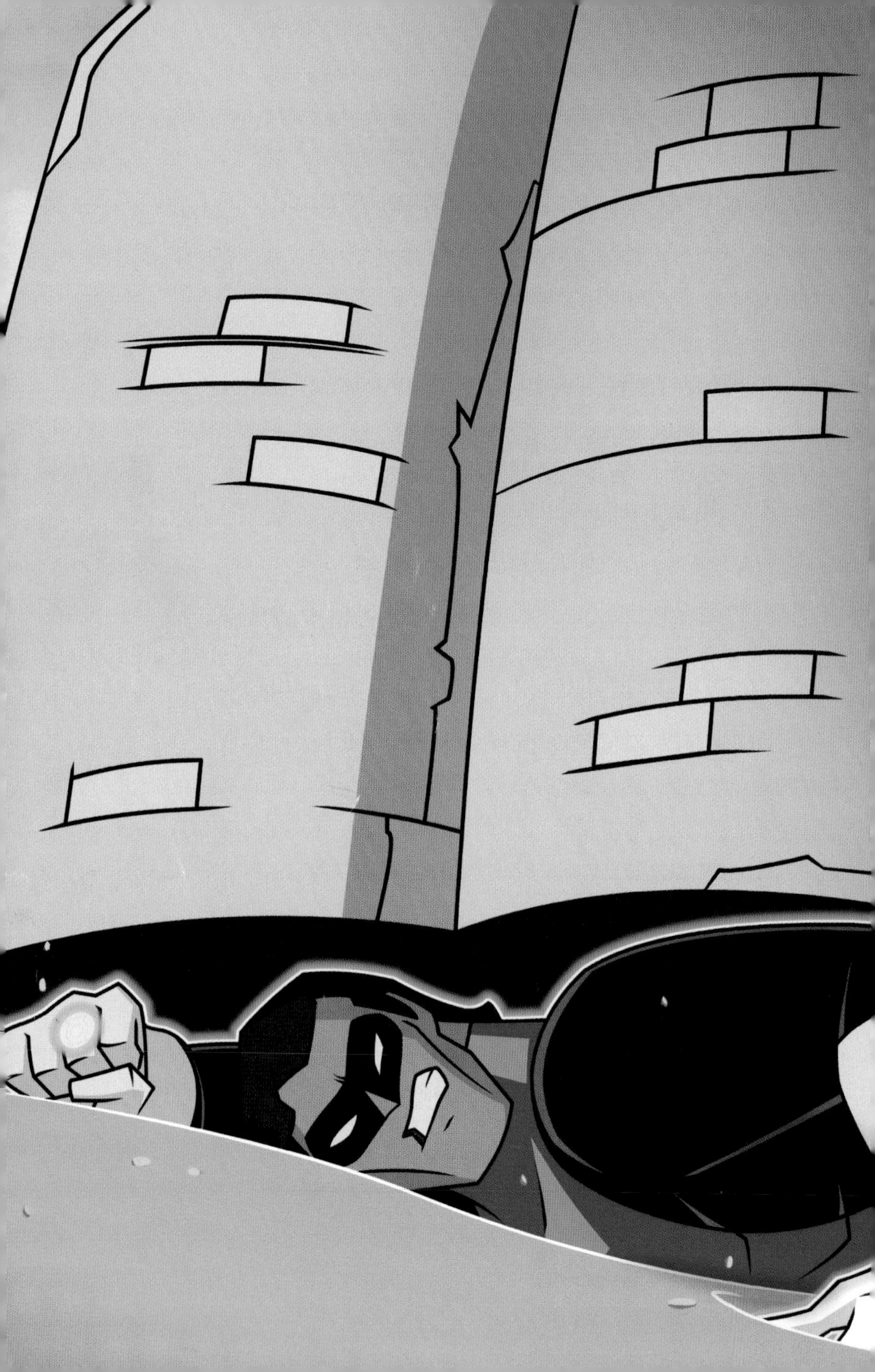

Hal tried to think of something he could create to help him escape. Vandal Savage was laughing on top of the Sphinx, making Green Lantern grit his teeth.

What was it Savage had said? the hero tried to recall. *The Sphinx is a being of pure energy. If the beast can't be hurt, maybe it can still be disrupted.*

Green Lantern knew that large things weren't always the most powerful. Tiny atoms, when used in unexpected ways, could destroy entire galaxies.

Despite his difficulty breathing, Green Lantern forced himself to calm down. He sent out a stream of energy that was only one atom wide. The beam looped multiple times around the Sphinx's head. Then the super hero made that thin strand of energy vibrate as quickly as possible.

He twirled the beam around the creature so fast that it couldn't be seen.

For a few moments, nothing happened. Without being able to breathe, Green Lantern struggled to remain conscious. He focused on keeping the atom-thin strand of energy spinning as fast as he could.

Then the Sphinx's head suddenly warped, changing shape like a balloon losing air. The spinning atoms were blocking the Sphinx's energy, just as Green Lantern had hoped!

The Sphinx reared back, almost tossing Vandal Savage from his mount.

Green Lantern pulled free of the Sphinx's claws and zoomed into the air. He soared out of the beast's pouncing range.

"Disrupting his energy?" Savage mocked. "You're not strong enough to completely shut him down!"

"Maybe not," Green Lantern replied, "but I can make him useless until you surrender." He concentrated on keeping the strand of atoms spinning rapidly around the Sphinx's head. *WHIR-WHIR-WHIR-WHIR!*

The Sphinx tossed his head around like he was trying to get rid of a pesky fly.

"Power levels at 30%," Green Lantern's ring reported, "and dropping rapidly."

Green Lantern had used up more power than he'd expected creating the dragon. Now the energy was draining too quickly. He couldn't keep this up for long.

"Surrender?" Savage bellowed. "You haven't seen anything yet!"

ROOAAARRR!! The Sphinx opened his eyelids wide. The glow of his eyes became blindingly bright.

Then the Sphinx shot two sizzling laser beams at Green Lantern.

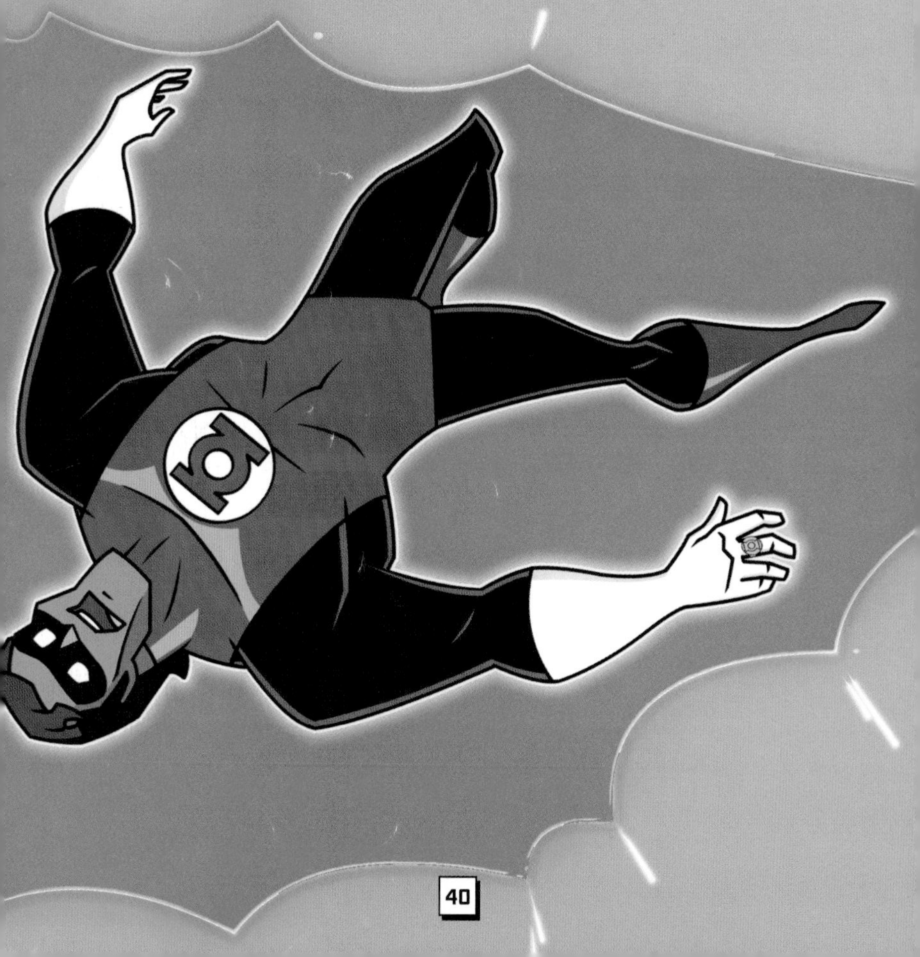

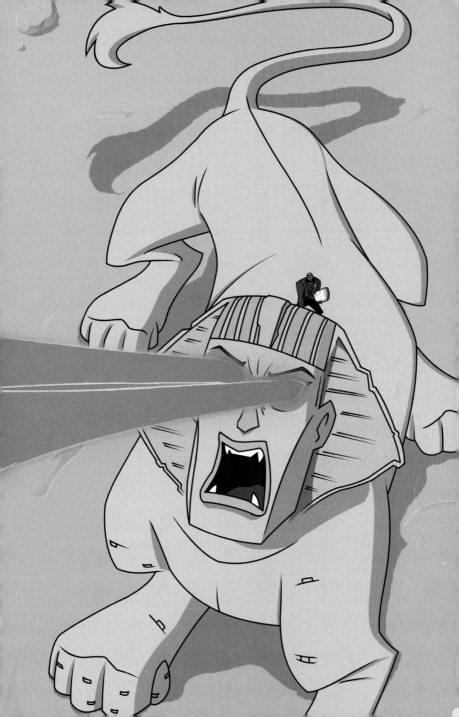

Green Lantern hadn't expected an ancient creature like the Sphinx to shoot lasers out of his eyes. **KA-BOOM!**

The beams hit him square in the chest. His force field protected him from terrible damage. Still, he was knocked backward, flinging out of control.

The hero slammed into one of the Great Pyramids and slid down the side. He pumped up his force field to full power to avoid worse damage if he got hit again.

"Now finish him!" Savage hollered.

Green Lantern leaped to the side to avoid being fried by another blast of lasers. He soared back into the sky, swooping around to make himself harder to hit. Then Green Lantern flipped in the air to avoid another laser attack.

Before he could get his bearings, a follow-up blast winged him. *ZZAPPPPPP!* His strengthened force field absorbed the beam, but still it rattled him.

"Power levels at 10%," the ring warned.

Green Lantern knew he wouldn't survive a direct hit. He had to do something fast.

"We've got him on the run!" Savage shouted. He laughed, raising the tablet over his head and shaking it triumphantly.

The tablet! Green Lantern remembered.

Savage had used the tablet to animate the Sphinx, so maybe it could be used to stop him. Green Lantern was sure the Sphinx would block any direct attack on the tablet. But maybe he wouldn't expect an indirect assault.

Green Lantern quickly created the basic shape of a X-211 scramjet around himself.

"Get him!" Savage bellowed. "He's trying to escape!"

Green Lantern had no thought of escaping. He soared across the desert in the X-211, quickly picking up speed. Then he blazed back toward Savage and the Sphinx, gunning the accelerator.

Steering the X-211 between two laser blasts, Green Lantern brought the ship low over Vandal Savage and the Sphinx.

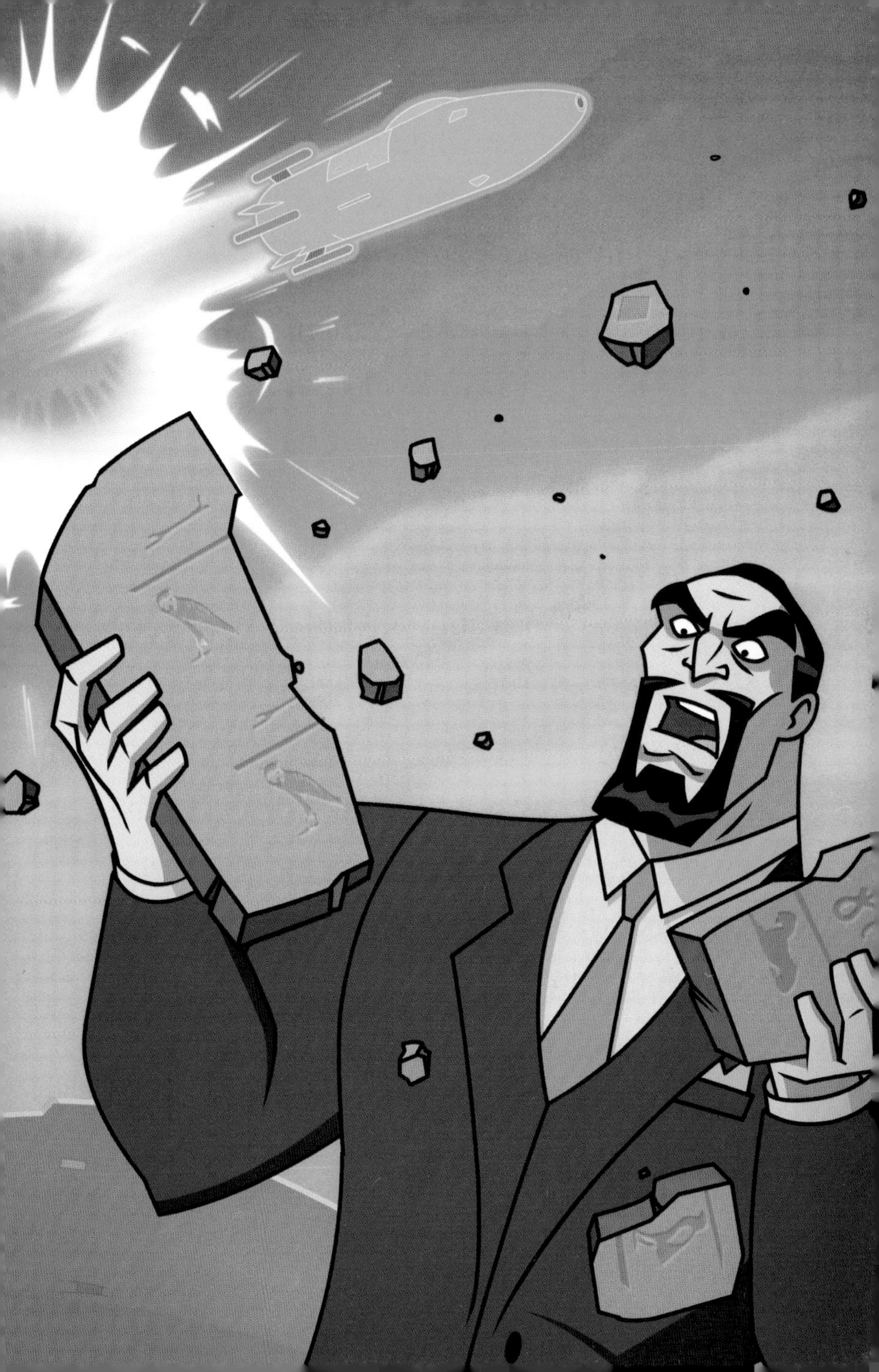

The Sphinx crouched to pounce at the scramjet . . . just as the X-211 broke the sound barrier. *WHOOOOSH!*

The sonic boom was deafening. Shock waves echoed across the desert. Right beneath the X-211, the blast had been the strongest.

The force of the sonic boom didn't affect the Sphinx, but it shattered the tablet into tiny chunks of rock. And it knocked Vandal Savage unconscious.

With the tablet destroyed, the Sphinx turned back to stone. He appeared exactly the same as he had before Savage had animated him.

Green Lantern let the X-211 dissolve and flew down toward Savage.

"Power levels at 2%," reported the ring.

The villain was just regaining consciousness.

"What happened?" Savage moaned. He spotted the shards of the tablet, and the stone Sphinx. "No," he gasped.

"Yes," Green Lantern said. "From the air, I saw that your lair is buried under the original location of the Sphinx. Maybe being immortal won't be such a benefit to you if you're trapped in there for eternity."

Green Lantern picked up Savage and dropped him into the underground hideout. Ignoring Savage's howls of protest, the hero raised the Sphinx statue and slid it into its original place.

As the entrance closed, Savage shouted, "I will have my revenge, Green Lantern! No prison can hold me!"

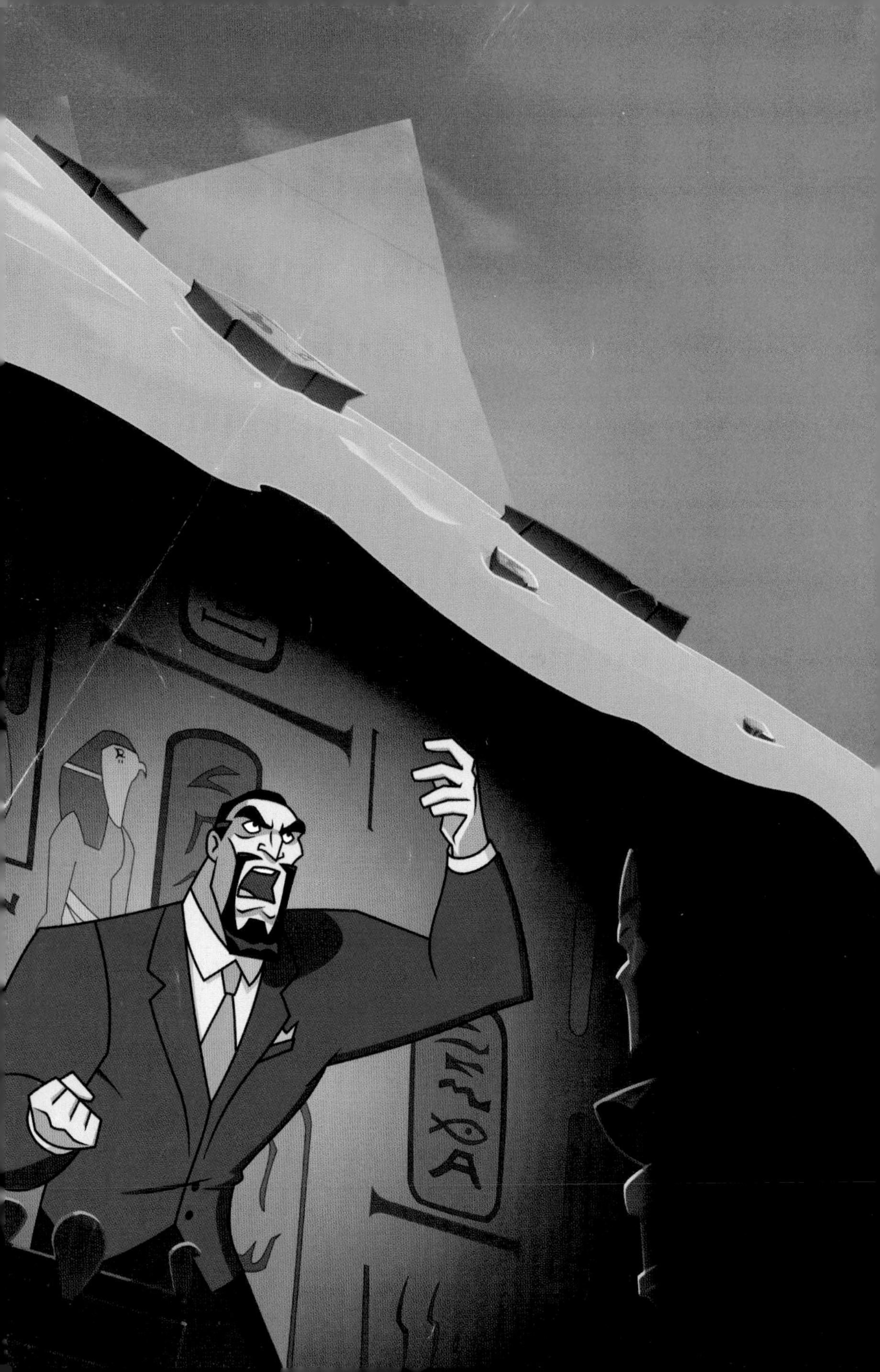

"Power levels at 0%," Green Lantern's ring reported after the Sphinx was in place.

"Oh, well," Green Lantern said. "I guess I'll be taking an airplane back home to California."

But that was fine with him. With his powers or without, Hal loved to fly.

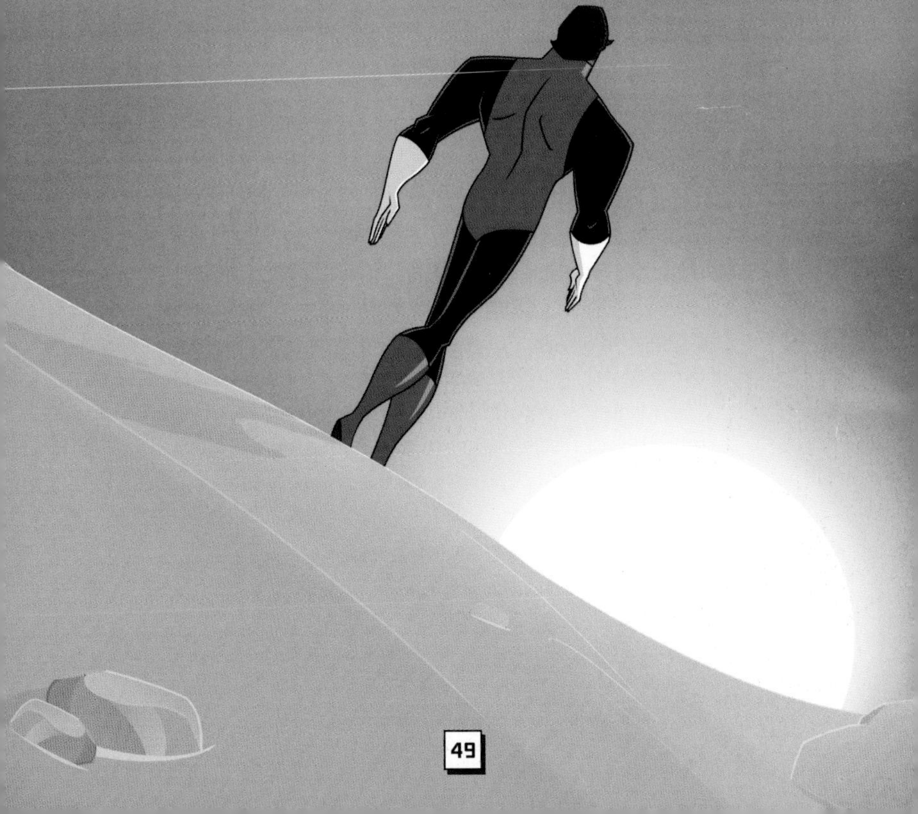

VANDAL SAVAGE

REAL NAME: Vandar Adg

OCCUPATION: Villain

HEIGHT: 5' 10" **WEIGHT:** 170 lbs.

EYES: Brown   **HAIR:** Black

POWERS/ABILITIES: Unmatched strategist and scientist; brilliant mind; immortality; years and years of experience in the dark arts.

BIOGRAPHY

Vandal Savage has lived for more than 50,000 years! During the Prehistoric Era, the Cro-Magnon warrior was exposed to powerful radiation from a meteorite. The event gave Vandal immortality and a highly advanced intellect. As years passed, Vandal used his powers for evil, befriending hateful emperors and murderous dictators in every era throughout history. In modern times, he continues his never-ending fight against the powers of good, seeking to destroy the World's Greatest Super Heroes and anyone who tries to stop him.

In the Prehistoric Era, Vandal Savage was a caveman chief known as Vandar Adg. He led the Cro-Magnon Blood Tribe, which ruled the region later known as Europe.

Throughout history, Vandal Savage worked with many cold-hearted rulers and villains including Ghengis Khan, Vlad the Impaler, Blackbeard, Napoleon, and Jack the Ripper.

For thousands of years, Vandal developed both his body and mind. He trained with the greatest fighters ever known and went to the best schools, making his combat skills and intellect second to none.

Vandal is the father of thousands of children including a daughter named Scandal Savage, who also possesses immortality.

BIOGRAPHIES

J. E. Bright has had more than 50 novels, novelizations, and non-fiction books published for children and young adults. He is a full-time freelance writer, living in a tiny apartment in the SoHo neighborhood of Manhattan with his good, fat cat, Gladys, and his evil cat, Mabel, who is getting fatter.

Dan Schoening was born in Victoria, B.C., Canada. From an early age, Dan has had a passion for animation and comic books. Currently, Dan does freelance work in the animation and game industry and spends a lot of time with his lovely little daughter, Paige.

GLOSSARY

archeology (ar-kee-OL-uh-jee)—studying the past by digging up old buildings and objects and carefully examining them

atmosphere (AT-muhss-feer)—the mixture of gases that surrounds a planet

friction (FRIK-shuhn)—the force that slows down objects when they rub against each other

hieroglyphics (hye-ur-uh-GLIF-iks)—writing used by ancient Egyptians, made up of pictures and symbols

incinerated (in-SIN-uh-ray-tuhd)—burned to ashes

Mach (MAHK)—a unit for measuring an aircraft's speed; Mach 1 equals the speed of sound.

pharaoh (FAIR-oh)—the title of kings of ancient Egypt

pictogram (PIK-tuh-gram)— an ancient or prehistoric drawing or painting on stone

sarcophagus (sahr-KAH-fuh-guhss)—a stone coffin

DISCUSSION QUESTIONS

1. Vandal Savage said that the stone tablet belonged to him. Do you think he deserved to control the powerful artifact? Why or why not?

2. How do Hal's skills as a test pilot help him as a Green Lantern?

3. Vandal Savage has lived for more than 50,000 years and experienced many different eras. If you could go back in time, what era would you choose and why?

WRITING PROMPTS

1. This story contains real-life places, buildings, and historical artifacts. Research and write down several facts about Egypt, the Sphinx, and mummies.

2. Write another story about Vandal Savage. Where will the villain show up next? How will he be defeated?

3. The Green Lantern ring can create anything its wearer imagines. If you had a ring, what would you will it to create? Write about your creation, and then draw a picture of it.

MORE NEW GREEN LANTERN ADVENTURES!

SUPER DC HEROES
GREEN LANTERN
ESCAPE FROM THE ORANGE LANTERNS

ESCAPE FROM THE ORANGE LANTERNS

SUPER DC HEROES
GREEN LANTERN
PRISONER OF THE RING

PRISONER OF THE RING

SUPER DC HEROES
GREEN LANTERN
RED LANTERNS' REVENGE

RED LANTERNS' REVENGE

SUPER DC HEROES
GREEN LANTERN
FEAR THE SHARK

SUPER DC HEROES
GREEN LANTERN
WEB OF DOOM

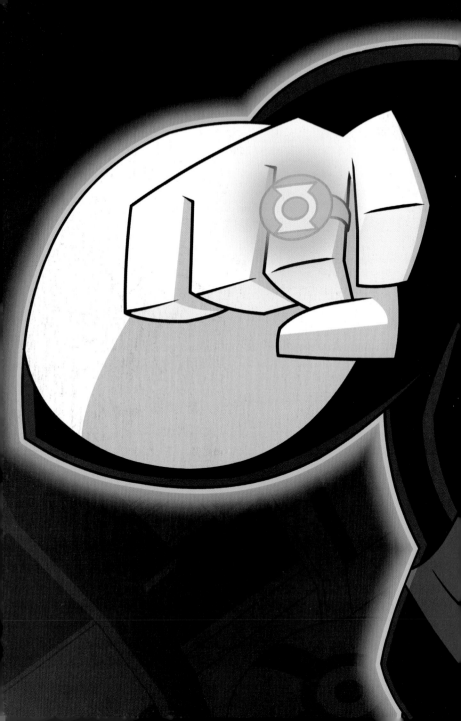

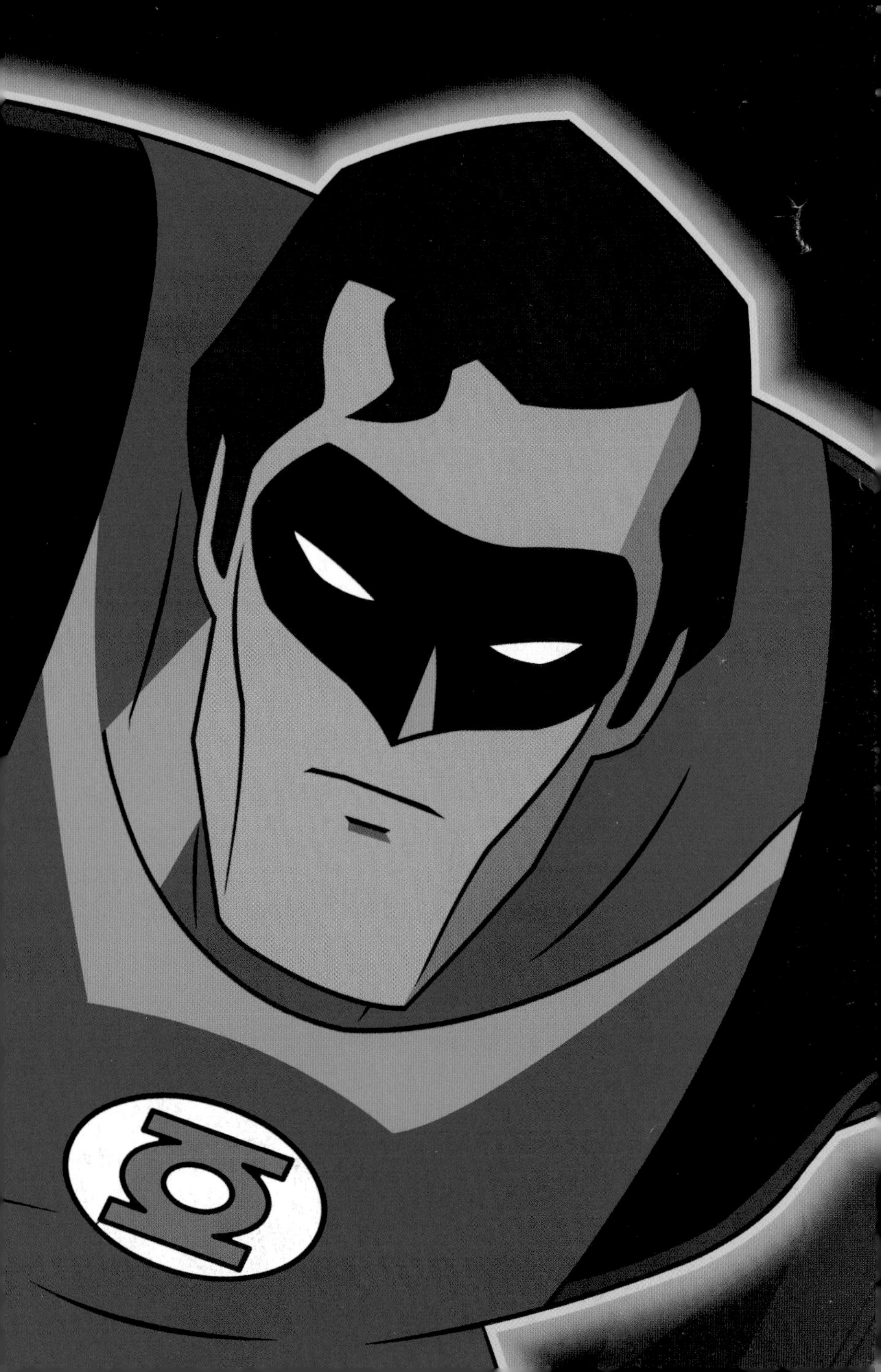